THE STORY OF
SNOW-WHITE AND THE
SEVEN DWARFS

The Brothers Grimm

THE STORY OF

Snow-White
and the
Seven Dwarfs

ILLUSTRATED BY

FRITZ WEGNER

HENRY Z. WALCK, INC.

NEW YORK

Library of Congress Cataloging in Publication Data
Grimm, Jakob Ludwig Karl, 1785-1863.
The story of Snow-White and the seven dwarfs.
(Walck fairy tales with historical notes)
SUMMARY: A princess takes refuge from her wicked
stepmother in the cottage of seven dwarfs.
[1. Folklore—Germany. 2. Fairy tales] I. Grimm,
Wilhelm Karl, 1786-1859, joint author. II. Wegner,
Fritz, illus. III. Title.
PZ8.G882Svs   398.2'2'0943 [E]   73-5973
ISBN 0-8098-1208-8

General Editor: Kathleen Lines

ISBN: 0-8098-1208-8
Library of Congress Catalog Card Number: 73-5973
Printed in the United States of America

Once upon a time the queen of a distant country sat sewing beside her window, and the frame of the window was of black wood called ebony. It was a day in mid-winter with snow falling like feathers from the sky, and through cracks and crannies snowflakes had drifted and lay upon the ebony window-sill.

As she sat at her work, looking out now and then at the snow-covered garden, the queen accidentally pricked her finger, and three drops of blood fell upon the snow. Seeing how bright the red blood looked against the white of the snow and the black of the window frame, the queen said, "Would that I had a child as white as snow, as red as blood and as black as ebony."

In time the queen's wish was granted. She had a beautiful baby daughter with skin as white as snow, lips as red as blood, and hair as black as ebony, and the child was given the name of Snow-White. And when the baby was born the queen died.

After a year had passed the king took to himself another wife. The new queen was beautiful but so vain and proud that she could not bear anyone else to be her equal in beauty. She had a magic looking-glass which hung upon the wall of her room, before which she would stand and say:

"Mirror, mirror on the wall
Who is the fairest of us all?"
And always the mirror answered:
"Thou art the fairest, Lady Queen."
Then she was content, for she knew the mirror always spoke the truth.

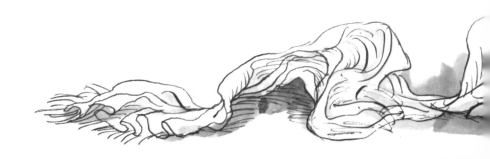

Meanwhile little Snow-White grew prettier all the time. When she was seven years old she was as beautiful as the bright day, and more beautiful than the queen herself.

One day when the queen stood before her looking-glass and said:

"Mirror, mirror on the wall

Who is the fairest of us all?"

The mirror answered:

"Thou wert the fairest, Lady Queen,

But Snow-White is fairer far, I ween."

This answer so shocked the queen that she became pale with anger and jealousy, and from that moment she hated the child.

Bitterness and envy grew in the queen's angry heart like rank weeds, giving her no peace, day or night. At last she could bear the sight of Snow-White no

longer, so she called a huntsman and said, "The child must die. Take her away into the forest so that I never set eyes on her again. Kill her and bring me back her heart as a token."

The huntsman had to obey. He took Snow-White by the hand and led her into the forest. But when he reached for his hunting knife Snow-White began to weep.

"Alas, dear huntsman," she cried, "Only spare my life, and I will run into the forest and never come home again."

The huntsman, touched by her tears and her beauty, had pity on her, and said,

"Run along then, you poor child."

And it seemed as though a stone had been rolled away from his heart, so thankful was he to let her go, even though he was sure that wild beasts would soon devour her.

At that moment a young boar came in sight. The huntsman killed it, cut out its heart and took that to the queen as proof that Snow-White was dead. The wicked woman cooked the heart and ate it thinking that was the end of Snow-White for ever.

Little Snow-White was now quite alone in the silent forest. She felt very frightened. The great trees towered above her and the movement and rustle of their leaves added to her terror. She began to run, struggling through the undergrowth of bushes and brambles, and bruising her feet on the rough and stony ground. As she ran the wild animals sprang past her or followed after, but none did her any harm.

At last, towards evening, she came to a little house, and she went inside to rest, for her legs could carry her no further. There was no one at home but the cottage was as neat and clean as could be. Everything in it was very small.

A little table stood in the middle of the room covered with a clean white cloth and already laid for a meal. There were seven little plates, each with its little spoon and knife and fork, and beside each plate was a little loaf of bread, and a little beaker of wine. Against the wall seven little beds stood side by side in a row, all with clean covers and neatly made. Snow-White, because she was so hungry and thirsty, ate a little food from each plate, took a little piece of bread

from each loaf and drank a sip of wine from each goblet, for she did not want to take all of one person's share. Then, being very tired, she got into one of the little beds. But it was not comfortable, so she tried the next one, but it was too short, and none was right for her until she came to the seventh; and there she lay down, commended herself to God and at once fell fast asleep.

When it was dark the masters of the cottage returned. They were seven dwarfs who worked all day digging for gold and copper in the heart of the nearby mountain. After they had lit their seven little lamps they saw at once that someone had been in their cottage, for everything was not as they had left it.

The first dwarf said:
"Who has been sitting in my chair?"
And the second dwarf said:
"Who has been eating from my plate?"
And the third:
"Who has been cutting with my knife?"
And the fourth:
" Who has been breaking my bread?"
And the fifth:
"Who has been eating with my spoon?"
And the sixth:
"Who has been using my fork?"
And the seventh:
"Who has been drinking my wine?"

17

The first dwarf then noticed the impression Snow-White made when she lay down upon his bed, and cried,

"Someone has been sleeping in my bed!"

The others came running and they said:

"Why, someone has been in our beds too!"

The seventh dwarf when he looked at his bed found Snow-White sleeping there. He called his companions who crowded round in astonishment. Then they fetched their lamps so that the light fell upon Snow-White.

"Gracious Heaven! What a beautiful child," they said softly to each other.

And their hearts were so filled with joy that they took great care not to wake her. The seventh dwarf, in whose bed she lay, slept with his comrades, spending an hour with each in turn, and in this way passed the night.

In the morning when Snow-White awoke and saw the seven dwarfs, she felt very frightened. But the dwarfs were friendly, and were gentle when they asked her name and how she had come to their house.

"My name is Snow-White," she answered. And she told them how the queen wished to be rid of her, how the huntsman had spared her life, and how she had run all the day through the forest, without food or rest, until at last she had reached their cottage.

The dwarfs felt compassion for the poor child, and said:

"You may stay here with us and want for nothing if you will be our housekeeper. Will you cook and bake and wash and make the beds; and mend and sew and spin, and see that everything is clean and tidy?"

"Oh, yes, with all my heart," Snow-White answered. So she lived with the seven dwarfs and kept their house in order.

Every morning they set out with mattocks and spades to dig and delve in the mountains for gold and copper and other precious ore, and when they came home at night Snow-White had supper ready for them. And so time passed. But during all the daylight hours the maiden was alone, so the dwarfs warned her to be on her guard.

"Never open the door to anyone," they said. "The wicked queen will surely find out that you are here and will try to harm you."

Meanwhile the queen, thinking that Snow-White was dead, exulted in the belief that no one in the land could match her in beauty.

But one day she stood before her looking-glass, as of old, and said:

"Mirror, mirror on the wall
Who is the fairest of us all?"
The mirror replied:
"Thou wert the fairest, Lady Queen,
But Snow-White is fairer far, I ween.
Mid the forest, darkly green,
She lives with dwarfs—the hills between."

The queen was astounded and terribly angry. She knew then that the huntsman had deceived her, for the mirror could not lie, and that Snow-White was still alive. Day and night she wondered how she could make an end of her. Then she thought of a plan. She put on rough clothes, painted her face and made herself look like an old woman, and carrying a pedlar's tray she followed the road over seven hills until she reached the house of the seven dwarfs.

She knocked on the door, at the same time crying, "Fine wares for sale! Fine wares for sale!"

Snow-White came to the window.

"What have you to sell, my good woman?"

"Fine things, pretty things," answered the old woman and held up laces of gay plaited silk.

"Surely there can be no harm in opening the door to this honest soul," said Snow-White to herself. So she unbarred the door and bought the pretty laces.

"Good gracious, child," exclaimed the old woman, "What a state you are in. Come let me lace your bodice properly."

Snow-White, suspecting no harm, stood while the pedlar put in the new laces. But the old woman laced so fast, and laced so tightly that Snow-White could not breathe. She grew pale and fell senseless to the floor.

The eyes of the wicked queen sparkled with glee.

"Now I am the fairest in the land," she said, and hurried away.

In the evening the dwarfs were shocked to find their dear Snow-White lying as though dead upon the floor. Gently they picked her up and saw her tight bodice.

As soon as they cut through the lacing Snow-White began to breathe again, and in a little while could tell them what had happened.

The dwarfs said:

"You may be sure the old pedlar woman was none other than the queen herself."

And they warned her again not to let anyone into the house when they were not with her.

As soon as she reached home, the queen went to her mirror.

"Mirror, mirror on the wall
Who is the fairest of us all?"

The mirror replied:

"Thou wert the fairest, Lady Queen,
But Snow-White is fairer far, I ween.
Mid the forest, darkly green,
She lives with dwarfs—the hills between."

The queen almost fainted from fright. Snow-White had been brought back to life, and would know of her disguise. But jealousy did not allow her to rest. She made up her mind to kill Snow-White; and by witch-craft, in which she was skilled, she injected poison into a pretty ornamental comb. Then, assuming the disguise of a quite different old woman, she made her way over

the hills to the home of the seven dwarfs. Again she
knocked on the door and cried:

"Fine wares for sale!"

Snow-White put her head out of the window.

"Please go away," she cried. "I must not let anyone
in."

"But at least you can look," said the old woman, and she held up the poisoned comb.

Snow-White thought the comb so pretty and wanted it so much that she opened the door and bargained for it. When the old woman asked to dress her hair properly for once, Snow-White let her have her way. But the instant the comb touched her the poison began to work and she fell senseless at the old woman's feet. "You paragon of beauty, now you are done for," said the wicked queen. And she hurried away.

By good fortune the dwarfs came home early that day. At once they suspected that the queen had been

there. They raised Snow-White and searched for anything that might have harmed her. They found the comb and scarcely had they taken it out than she recovered and told them all that had happened.

Once again the dwarfs warned Snow-White to be on her guard against the queen, and they forbade her to let anyone into the cottage.

Back at the palace the queen stood before her looking-glass:

"Mirror, mirror on the wall
Who is the fairest of us all?"

The mirror answered as before:
"Thou wert the fairest, Lady Queen,
But Snow-White is fairer far, I ween.
Mid the forest, darkly green,
She lives with dwarfs—the hills between."

When the queen knew that once again Snow-White had escaped death, she shook and trembled with rage. "Snow-White shall surely die," she cried, "even if it costs me my life."

Then she went into a secret room where she could not be disturbed because no one else knew of it, and

here she made a very poisonous apple. Outwardly it
appeared ripe and juicy, and all who saw it would
want to eat it; but one bite would cause instant death.

When the apple was ready, the queen assumed the
guise of an old village woman, and taking a basket of
apples, set off for the house of the seven dwarfs.

Snow-White saw the apple-woman come and told
her to go away. "The seven dwarfs have forbidden me
to let anyone in," she said.

"That is nothing to me," said the old woman. "I can easily sell my apples elsewhere. But let me give you one as a present."

"No," said Snow-White. "I dare not take it."

"What, are you afraid of poison?" The old woman laughed. "Look," she said, "I'll cut the apple in two, you shall have the rosy cheek and I will eat the other one."

Now the apple was so cunningly made that only the red side was poisonous. And while she was speaking the old woman halved the apple and began to eat it.

Snow-White felt a great desire for the delicious-looking fruit, and when she saw the woman eating she hesitated no longer but held out her hand and took the poisoned half. However before she had taken more than one bite, she fell down dead.

The wicked queen laughed in triumph. "Red as blood, white as snow, black as ebony, this time the dwarfs cannot bring you back to life."

At home in the palace, the queen stood before her looking-glass.

"Mirror, mirror on the wall
Who is the fairest of us all?"

And this time the mirror answered:
"Thou art fairest, Lady Queen."

Then the queen's jealous heart was at rest—at least, as much at rest as a jealous heart could ever be.

That evening when the dwarfs came home they found Snow-White lying quite still upon the floor.

They picked her up and looked everywhere for anything which could have done her harm. They undid her clothes and combed her hair. They washed her face with wine and with water, but all in vain. Snow-White was dead and the seven dwarfs could not bring her back to life.

They laid her body on a bier, and watched and wept beside it for three days. Then they would have buried Snow-White, but they could not bear to for she looked as though she merely slept. Her skin was as white as snow, her lips as red as blood and her hair as black as ebony.

"We cannot put her away into the dark ground," they said amongst themselves.

Instead, they had a coffin of transparent glass made for Snow-White so that she could be seen from all sides. And on the top, in letters of gold, they wrote her name and that she was a king's daughter.

The dwarfs carried the glass coffin out to the hillside, and one at a time they kept watch day and night.

Snow-White lay a long time in the glass coffin but her appearance did not change. Her skin was still as white as snow, her lips as red as blood and her hair as black as ebony. She looked as though she were asleep.

Now by chance a king's son came that way. He read the words written in gold on the glass coffin, and saw beautiful Snow-White lying within.

He said to the dwarfs:

"Let me have Snow-White in her glass coffin and I will pay whatever you ask."

But they said:

"We will not part with Snow-White for all the gold in the world."

The prince said, "Then give her to me, for I cannot live without her. I will honour her and guard her as my greatest treasure, and she will be dearer to me than anything in the world."

The good dwarfs, pitying his distress, gave Snow-White to the prince. He ordered his servants to lift the glass coffin shoulder high and carry it to his father's kingdom.

Now as they journeyed it happened that one of the servants stumbled over a tree-stump and shook the coffin. This jolting set free the piece of poisoned apple that had lodged in Snow-White's throat. In a little while she opened her eyes, pushed back the glass top and sat up, alive and well.

"Great Heaven!" she cried, "Where am I?"

Full of joy the prince answered. "You are with me, and you are dearer to me than the whole world."

He told her all that had happened, and then he said,

"I love you with all my heart. Will you come with me to my father's house, and be my bride?"

Snow-White looked on him and loved him, and agreed to go with him.

Their marriage took place amid royal pomp and great splendour and a magnificent celebration followed. Among the guests invited to the wedding party was Snow-White's old enemy, the wicked queen.

She was already dressed for the occasion, when, by habit, she stood in front of her looking-glass.

"Mirror, mirror on the wall
Who is the fairest of us all?"
The mirror answered:
"Thou wert the fairest, Lady Queen,
But the prince's bride is fairest now, I ween."

At these words the queen was beside herself with fear and jealousy, and did not know what to do. At first she would on no account attend the wedding party; but then she felt she must see the prince's bride for herself. When the queen entered the ballroom and

recognised Snow-White (whom she had done to death, as she thought, long ago) she stood rooted to the spot in terror. But there was no escape from the terrible fate awaiting her.

Iron slippers had been heated on the fire and were

now carried in by tongs and placed before her. The wicked woman had to put on the red-hot shoes and dance in them till she fell down dead.

Snow-White and her prince lived happily for the rest of their lives, and they never forgot their good little friends, the seven dwarfs.

When the old king died the prince became king in his stead, and he ruled wisely and well with Snow-White as his queen.

THE STORY OF
SNOW-WHITE AND THE SEVEN DWARFS

'Snow-White' (*Schneewitchen*) was among the first of the traditional stories the Brothers Grimm collected from the peasants of Hesse in 1812; and, called 'Snowdrop', it was also in the very first selection of tales from Grimm to be translated into English:

> *German Popular Stories*, Translated from the *Kinder und Haus-Märchen*, collected by M. M. Grimm, From Oral Tradition. Published by C. Baldwyn, Newgate Street, LONDON 1823.

A reproduction of the title page (above) is shown in Harvey Darton's *Children's Books in England* (plate V), and a facsimile paper-bound edition of the book was published in 1971, by the Scolar Press.

Neither translator nor illustrator is named, nor the author of Preface and Notes. But since Cruikshank signed his etchings there could have been no doubt that they were his. He was well-known, and, as Darton states, 'one of the best artists of the day—then in the prime of his long career'.

Later, evidence disclosed that Edgar Taylor and 'a circle of relatives' made the translation and that Taylor had written both Preface and Notes. Edgar Taylor, on his own, translated and annotated a further selection of 'popular' German tales and this book, published in 1826, was also illustrated by Cruikshank.

Forty years on (1868) both series were reissued in one volume at the request of Ruskin for his 'favourite old stories in their earliest English form': *German Popular Stories* With illustrations after the original designs of George Cruikshank Edited by Edgar Taylor With Introduction by John Ruskin, M.A. (from the title page)

In the Introduction Ruskin sets forth, at some length, his views on the value of traditional literature, and deplores adapted versions of the old tales, and the moral fanciful stories and family stories then being 'presented to the acceptance of the Nursery'. Appropriately (printed at the end of the book) and supporting Ruskin's argument there is Sir Walter Scott's letter to Edgar Taylor containing the often quoted: 'Truth is, I would not give one tear shed over Little Red Riding Hood for all the benefit to be derived from a hundred histories of Jemmy Goodchild. Edinburgh, January 16th, 1823.'

The Advertisement, by John Campden Hotton, shows that the importance of Cruikshank's etchings (twenty-two for the fifty-five stories) was another reason for the 'faithful reprint'. These were in great demand by collectors being 'the most prized of all the fine works of the great master'. Cruikshank made no illustrations for 'The Twelve Dancing Princesses', 'Briar Rose', 'Little Brother and Sister' and other tales of a magical romantic nature, and none for 'Snow-White' either.

The basic plot of 'Snow-White' has incidents in common with other popular stories, but several unique constituents—the magic looking-glass, the recurring words 'white as snow, red as blood and black as ebony', the little dwarfs in their little house with tiny furniture and fittings—give it a special enchantment. It has been included in almost every reputable collection of 'favourite' tales since that first selection and first translation so many years ago. It is strange that there should be families today who know the story only in Walt Disney's version, or in others almost equally different from the original.

This new edition has been produced in response to persistent requests for the *traditional* story in a form suitable for younger children. Fritz Wegner, drawing with imaginative insight and keeping young readers in mind, has made a truly 'fairy tale' picture-book.

The text has been assembled from a number of sources. I have relied most on a new literal translation (made for me from an authoritative German edition) which I compared with a number of early English versions and translations, and then, rather like Snow-White at the dwarfs' table, took this and that from here and there. I have given an explanation of how the drops of blood could fall upon snow; have substituted 'heart' for the German 'liver and lung'; and, after the wicked queen is finished off in traditional fashion, and by 'the truly Northern punishment of being obliged to dance in red-hot slippers or shoes', I have put in a happy ending—surely only to be expected. Otherwise any rewriting has been negligible. The first translators left out details of the wicked woman's death, softening it to, 'she choked with passion, fell ill, and died'. However to most children (particularly the young ones!) her fate is merely 'the wages of sin', the just reward for evil plans and deeds.

I should like to express my gratitude to Herta Ryder for her translation and also for her help and interest in interpreting the exact meaning of unusual or colloquial German expressions.

Since this story is one which is heard, or read, and enjoyed at several different ages in childhood, it seems unfortunate if children do not, from the very first, meet Snow-White and the seven dwarfs in the original version and the folk-setting recorded and described by the Brothers Grimm.

KATHLEEN LINES